Wo
the Railroad

Characters

Worker 1

Worker 2

Dinah the Train

Worker 3

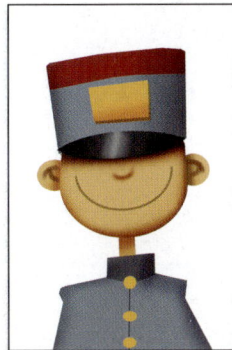

Captain

Setting

A train station

Picture Words

station

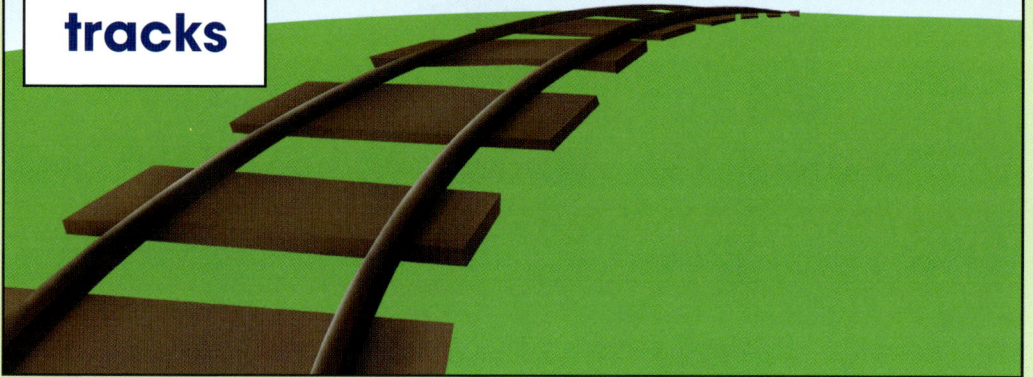

tracks

Sight Words

go	**here**	**I**	**let's**
see	**the**	**too**	**you**

train

whistle

Enrichment Words

blowing

railroad

wash

water

Worker 1: The train!

Worker 2: I see the train.

Dinah the Train: Toot toot.

Toot

Worker 3: I hear the train.

Dinah: Toot toot.

Captain: I can hear the whistle blowing. The train is coming into the station.

Toot

Worker 1: Look!

Worker 3: The train is here.

Captain: I love working on the railroad. I could work here all day long.

Worker 1: Yes!

Worker 2: Me, too.

Worker 3: Let's work!
Get some water.

Worker 2: Here is water!

Worker 3: Wash the train.

Worker 1: Get more water!

Worker 3: Wash the tracks.

Captain: Good job, everyone! Now let's have fun. Let's go for a ride on the train.

Worker 1: Let's go!

Captain: Wait! We can not go yet. Dinah needs to blow her horn first.

Worker 2: Blow, Dinah.

Worker 1: Blow.

Worker 3: Won't you blow, Dinah?

Captain: Come on, Dinah, blow your horn!

Dinah: Toot toot!

Worker 2: Yay!

Worker 3: Let's go, Dinah!

The End